Ameri(k/c)a

a

sort of

pseudo-reality

r.g. vasicek

I am an alien among you. I make notes in my notebooks because I... Eat your words. Eat! The feast of language. We must keep it simple. Ordinary language...I want it to be unfinished...I want the fragments. Are you listening? Bend over...I've got a notebook for you...a notebook for your ass-pocket! This war notebook must show... what? The scribbles of thought? Spirals of nonsense? Stick-figure feelings? Are we at war with the State of Things? Am I propagandizing? I smell the piss of a dog. I am a lo-fi novelist. KDP gets me excited: Checking your trim size...I remember a girlfriend. She had firmware in her briefs. Daylight ass versus soft white ass. What is it I want to say? Perhaps it is not me. The notebook writes itself. Everybody is scrambling under the concrete ruins as bombs drop. Brutalist

architecture. Bauhaus. Where is
my house?

No house. We linger in
courtyards. We huddle under
blankets. We thirst. I thirst.
Hungry ghost. Insatiable phantom.
What is my religion? Do I
believe in ghosts? The holy
ghost? This notebook is made
of paper & ink. A few words...
for you. I am nothing else.
I pass through this moment.
Passerby. A glimpse...a blink...a
blink...Augenblink. 8 April is
an infinite day. Solar eclipse.
Human beings & 3D glasses. The
war is out there. You can't be
from anywhere. You've got to be
from nowhere. I wanted writing to
be more than it is....and already
it is everything. What did I
mean? In the beginning of the
beginning. Writing changes...and
you change. I keep looking across
the street. What intrigues me
so? It takes me a moment...until I
realize... she has an excited ass!
Vectors of movement. Chaos. The
quantum foam. My roommate & I

attack each other's language. My name is not I. I is a substitute for me.(I) no longer trust images. What else is there? The eyeball sees. Signs. I am without language.
I.

.

.

I.

I am.

Am I.

I like the rain...now I have to deal with the sun. Are you satisfied with your wireless? What is culture? Are you hungry? Are you starving? Enough is enough...isn't it? How do you get anywhere with yr thoughts? Are your balls itchy? Is your cunt wet? Are you satisfied with the seating arrangement? Are you in need of a buzzcut? Get out of my way...I am writing! Hostile nation state...I am a headache...a migraine...are we tennis players?...lobbers...overhead slammers...Alabama slammers? Are we textual? Are we in a textual position? My eyeballs are optical testicles... her ass glitches in my face...she comes on my quivering dome...enough is not enough...I want more...every dinner is a last supper...yelp yelp yelp...the puppy is biting...I am yawning...trying to sleep... easier here...in our dreams & nightmares...war landscape outside...rubble...a metropolis in ruins...men riding around on bicycles...looking for a can of soup...there is no President... there is no Commander...not anymore...we are just people here...human beings...Neanderthals in the machine age...earbuds popping out...reality disturbed... yes...the earth...the sea...the sky... we get lost in each other's mindscapes...get out...get out! I gave her a sneak peak of my cock... she gave me an Augenblick of her pussy...You want me to

lecture in your lecture center...
and why? The neolithic &
mesolithic occupation of my
thoughts...I preoccupy the
occupier. A trick for the
Cyclops. I thought I was better
behaved. Amerika teaches me. a
Toyota pickup truck...McGuinness
Boulevard & Humboldt Street &
Meeker Avenue. Enough of your
punctuation. Enough of your
micr(o)quantum grammar. Erotic
horror & dark fantasy. She puts
an e-collar on my cock. A little
zap when I get too close to
Czech pussy. Are you a New
Yorker? Are you a Long Islander?
Are you a Czechoslovakian? We
meet up at the Partridge Pub.
Notebook 1 is the hardest
notebook to write. I keep writing
& writing & writing. You keep
reading & reading & reading. Do
not give up! You can do this. I
believe in you. Are we telepaths
in the digital age? Is a mobile
phone yr "anchor to
civilization"? Are you
adequately charged? Wittgenstein
says description not explanation!

Do you agree? I keep an eyeball on the word count. I get paid by the wormhole. Portal opened. Is your nervous system triggered by silence? "What are you thinking about, Mr. Zig?" "Eternity." "Is that possible? "I think so." "And how is it going?" "I will let you know when I get there." Writer. Are you writing? It is 10:31pm. Do you even give a fuck? I am A.I...doorlatch... keys...what what what...hurtling across the surface of superhighways...towards airports...& beyond...a surfer of surfaces...Yes... well...the heat is coming...the burn...the planet is cooling. Yes...the intimacy of nothingness...I kiss Death's wet lips...I am a surfer of the abyss... Why are we the tax bucket for the planet? The village is a village, is it not? Are you not a villager? The potato fields. The wheat fields. The slaughterhaus. Who are you? if you are...if you are...The motor scooters of tomorrow running on human thoughts. We reengineer the network. The system is beyond control. It must be so hard to be a person. Are you a fucking person? I think so. Kamila. She opens her legs. Her sex glistens with wetness. I unroll a latex ring on my cock & approach. She lays on her stomach. My cock opening the rims of anuses. Human thoughts are forever...I write because I want to become something else? The "thought-sounds" I hear! I am...just starting...to become...after a half century & more. My life is a mess...how can it be otherwise? Notebook 1 dissolves & recrystallizes. Are you a believer? Are you a notebook keeper? Tip of a tongue on an erect brown nipple...How do you put together a life? What are the components? What are the ingredients? Tits & tits & ass & tits...the eyeball squanders its ability to see. Balls of light. Luminescent. Translucent. What... am I...supposed to zoom-in on? Are you a writer of circumstance? A totality of circumstance? Semi-circle.

Circumcision. The Omphalos of the belly button. I take off my shirt. She takes off her jeans. Bottom of her thighs on my shoulders. I lick & lick & lick that pussy. She starts bucking. Squeezing my nose in her ass. My cock stirs. Wants some of the action. A vanilla & chocolate milk shake. Whipped cream everywhere. Sprinkles. Noise from a UFO. Cheskomorava, easy on the goulash... more dumplings please! Chesnek. Paprika. The army jacket. The boots. I trudged around the metropolis. Sifting through the ruins of human consciousness. Hey... we've got to get through this moment... we can do it... yeah? I can see the other side. I take a step. You take a step. We are getting closer. The horizon shimmers. The plasma walls we create inside our heads. We are phantasmagoric black boxes. Camera lucida. I see you seeing me. So real it seems. Am I right? Our asses painted with the brushes of Vermeer. I am naked again. Are you? What are the rules of the game? Is a notebook a notebook in a digital space? Are your digits used for fingering? Does your thumb plumb the depths? Are you a pie-eater? Blueberry? Raspberry? Goosenberry? Strawberry rhubarb? I am not even a real person. Are you fucking? How often? Who runs this country? I mean, really. What is the chain of command. Who operates the machines? Pushes the buttons. Rotates the dials. Easy on the warfare. Less is more. Maybe nothing at all. I am eager to explore the State or the Commonwealth of Massachusetts. Where is it, exactly? In proximity to my current coordinates. North by northwest? Is a compass necessary in the age of the great spin? The spiral & vortex through the galaxy. Notebook 1 is available for purchase in all vending machines. Right next to the Cape Cod potato chips with sea salt. Easy on the coinage. You will be poor in no time. Save something

for your anti-retirement. Defund
social security. Defund the Ponzi
war machine. What you get is
what you get. The kitchen scraps
of the oligarchs. The iron
shrapnel. The barbwire. Make
more noise. Bang the pots & pans.
Scream: I exist. The laundry
tumbles & tumbles & tumbles &
what is left of what you are? Did
you at least use a fabric
softener? A fragrant dryer
sheet? The electric dials no
longer function. You must
"estimate" time & space. Notebook
1 is getting fatter & fatter,
thicker & thinker. Words accrete.
Stick together. Mini-gravity
spheres. Spherules. Days keep
happening. Already 17 since the
8th. April is a luminescent mind
fuck. A festival of rain. Fog &
mist. Trees blossom. Notebook 1
is a microclimate. A geranium of
human thoughts at the End of the
Machine Age. We are tinkerers,
bricoleurs. Put on your welding
goggles. See the blue fire. I swig
a Wormtown at The Harp in
Amherst! Aye, I am the worm, the

wiggler. I dig holes under your wisteria. Spring is here, what hysteria! Notebook 1 is under pressure. Astoria, Queens is a vortex. The Omphalos of the Triboro Bridge. East River whirlpools & Hell Gate Bridge. I no longer know what I know. I erase. I forget. It gets better & better whatever this is. Notebook 1. A sanctuary. A safe space. A dangerous place. Dark magic. Black magic. Medieval contemplations. Self-flagellation. What are we? Prisoners? Refugees? Defectors? Is language even programmable? Is your zipper unzipped? Afternoon fuck? Are you afraid of Brutalist architecture? Concrete. Glass. You hurtle towards a thousand followers on X. Is it enough? Are twelve readers enough? The twelve Apostles of Hadley. A thirteenth in the UK. Possibly two in Prague. We engage with the engagers. Ask for no more. Ask for more. Ask ask ask. Questions are answers. Forget the exclamations. The "Shark Attack" sandwich at the Sugar Shack. The kielbasa sandwich at the Polish roadhouse. Mesmerized by nothingness... I stand before your language machine. The dryer is no longer drying. The tumbling machine. I am trying to escape my life. The vortex. The whirlpool. I eat & eat & eat. Are you satisfied with Notebook 1? Does it check off all the boxes? Chekov. Czech off. A buzzard circles. Eager for prey. The vultures of the mind. The vampires of Prague. The Castle on a hill. The Zhizzzzzzhkov TV radio tower & its giant climbing babies. Your memories serve the server. A machine-made thing. Cooled underground by nitrogen in a concrete bunker. Amerika is a bewilderment. It slaughters everything. Who are the button-pushers? Are we all button-pushers. You turn a dial... & what? She leapt out of my bed, a flying orgasm. A geyser of white-hot semen between her legs. I was a devil incarnate. A boll-weevil.

A Tasmanian devil. Maxwell's
demon. Nobody pushes buttons
anymore. The machine is in
control. She sends me postcards.
Asking for more in a faraway
land. I had no more to give. I
had no more to say. Every writer
begins & ends at the beginning.
The atomic bloom. A radioactive
flowering. Radio waves from an
icy moon orbiting Saturn. I
listen for the frequency. I turn a
knob. I press the scan button.
Static & more static. An
occasional blip. We are afraid of
extraterrestrial reality. The
possibility of our smallness.
Insignificance. We are crushed
like VW Beetles at the junkyard.
We are junkyard dogs. Circling
the wreckage. Mounting & fucking.
Tying the knot. A few howls at
the eclipsed moon. Nobody gets
very far. A few kilometers from
the village. A few kilometers
from the mouth of a limestone
cave. The People of the Karst. I
pick up a chainsaw & spin. We
slaughter trees. We plant
wisteria & hysteria. The ravens

circle. The gyre tightens. I am
the keeper of Notebook 1. Make no
mistake. It is on my shelf amidst
the other notebooks. Ink & paper
from the Machine Age. I pick
dandelions on the campus of
Hampshire College. Perhaps a
dandelion salad is in order. I
park the machine in a parking lot
in Massachusetts. The distance
from everything is exhilarating.

I begin Notebook 1 again in a
new paragraph. Because something
has changed. I do not know what.
It is change itself. A liquid
fluid thing. I am startled by the
development. I half-expected it.
I might even be what caused it?
The external/internal debate
rages on in academia & beyond.
We are creatures of circumstance.
And so much more. The white
space between paragraphs
scares me. The emptiness. The
void. The abyss. I might fall
through the crevasse with
my strapped-on crampons. My
black Converse Chuck Taylor
sneakers. My Australian boots.

Aye, I am a writer. Trying to summit the summit of all summits. Or perhaps I go underground. Deeper & deeper into a labyrinth of subterranean tunnels. The headlamp is appropriate. I switch it on. Wherever I am. Dayrunners. I save a buck or two on insurance. Keep the headlights on. Even beneath a scorching sun. Is it a black hole? An eclipse? Are we approaching the rim of an anus? The Egyptian god Anubis? I smash words together in a supercollider. I impress my friends. All twelve of my readers. The Apostles. A disproportionate representation in Hadley. And in the UK. Nevermind what the naysayers say. Say yes to yes. I am a speaker in a chamber. An electromagnetic chamber. An anechoic chamber. Ignore yourself. Your tell-tale heart beats too loud! I hear the sluice of blood in your arteries & veins. Quiet your mind. Calm your nervous system. Are you a flesh vessel of human feelings

& thoughts? Are you a litmus strip of the aether? Breathe. Breathe. Is there enough oxygen in this atmosphere? Are you an aficionado of the bathysphere? Are you an aquanaut? Are you a submersible pilot? Are you a fan of James Cameron's The Abyss? If you had to choose: Lovecraft or Poe? We go deeper & deeper into the abyss. Easier said than done. What? Everything. People talk. Blah blah blah. Prisoners of words. Prisoners of language. Arbeit Macht Frei. Was ist los? Wo ist diese Denken? Are you a thinker? Are you a thought-maker? Are you craving solitude. Is late April a carnival? Are you becoming who you are? Are you a toolmaker? Is your toolbox getting heavier? The adjustable wrench. Everything seems so promising. And then the bills start piling up. Who designed this system? In their own image? A machine-made machine? I fabricate reality.

Nothing has changed. And yet

I begin again. Are you ready
for tomorrow? Is it 1 hour &
3 minutes away? 10:57pm? The
people of Hadley sleep. Not the
people of Astoria, Queens. We are
night riders. Vampires. Valkyrie.
It feels impossible sometimes.
Whatever this is.

I drift.

Are you a speaker of human
language?

The language of bodily
movements.

Eye gestures.

Proximity.

She trains her mouth to form an O
around my cock.

We are almost there & we are not
there. A photo of Prague 1968.
The Russian tanks. The bloody
flag. An electric trolleybus is
on fire.

I explode.

My pants fall off. She hops on.
We make noise all night.

We sip coffee in the morning.
Each of us, a little shy.

I get dressed.

Her buttocks make an impression
on my retina.

Outside a concrete apartment
block, I shake my fist at the sky:
Why must I work in the factory!?

The VW Beetle fails to ignite.

I walk to the tram stop.

Let me put things in order. What
things? I do not know. Things.
Objects. Subjects. The Universe.
The Cosmos. Quite a mess, isn't
it? Disorder. Chaos. Utterly
utterly perfect.

I repeat myself. I am a repetition
machine.

Difference.

A difference engine.

Vroom! Vroom!
I am not a poet.

I am a keeper of notebooks. I am a notebookkeeper.

This is Notebook 1.

It begins like all the others... at the beginning.

If you do not think so, think again.

We approach an aggregate of text. I think I might call it a paragraph. If I can gather the courage. She says: "I have not written a thing since we got the dog." And here I sit at the typewriter, & I think: "Is that my fault?"
She vacuums & vacuums.

I type & type.

The 1st of May. What a thing to say. What a thing to believe.

Notebook 1 might last all summer.

The humidity will squeeze NYC into a droplet of sweat.

I must escape.

Iceland!

The North Pole!

I am here for the duration.

I am coming at you like a Kharkovchanka in Antarctica!

2nd of May. Are you satisfied? What is your situation? Are you comfortable? Agitated?

Is there war?

Yes.
Are you thinking?

I think so.

We sign things.

I guess because people die.

I will miss this Earth.
She liked my weirdness. I liked hers. We got naked & fooled around.

I need more cowbell.

I need more ass.

I need more everything.

Say yes.

Yes.

I was mad. I said: Fuck you, man. Fuck fuck fuck fuck you.

Space & light. I was laid: She gave it to me so fast & hard.

I lay there with a tear in my eye.

Every day I wake up & I am a beginner.

I watch her arc... orgasm running up & down her spine. She says she is my wife. I almost believe her.
Morning panic.

Getting places "on time".

Capitalism kicks in... the machine... the machine... the machine...

We are almost at 3K.

It must mean something.

Accretion.

Accumulation.

Notebook 1 is the fairest of the notebooks. It comes first. Has the nicest cover. The nicest ass.
We are war machines.

Each a one of us.

The computer makes me nervous.

Pen & ink drawings in the

margins of a notebook.

I sketch a schematic for a...

The ice in your ice coffee
is melting. Evidence of time?
Optical illusion? Passage of...
space... time?

I miss the fucking. The raw
winter fucks.

Are you a nightmare?

What happened to the paragraphs?

Did you disintegrate?

Are you testing out your police
eyeball?

Trying to read my manuscript at
a spooky distance?
We eclipsed 3K.

What a journey it has been.

Are you exhausted?

We must trudge higher.

Crampons might be necessary.

5:11 pm.
Paper. Ink. Human eyeballs.
A brain. A mind. Human
consciousness. Are we made of
fog & mist? A lighthouse emerges
from a rock in the sea. Terrible
waves batter the lighthouse. The
lighthousekeeper is nervous &
excited. Anything can happen:
Death & Nirvana.

5:32 pm.

5:33 pm.

It might rain later.

I find myself unable to pretend
to be a child anymore.
Even what I read.

I am getting older & older &
older.

Where are your feelings? Are
they in a lock box? A safety
deposit box?

What do I remember?... and why do I remember it?... these are questions that have been asked for thousands of years.

No answers are forthcoming.

Words are pictures.

Image-thoughts.

I think something keeps happening... and I am unable to say what it is.

We need space.

We need empty spaces.

I am an explorer.

Notebook 1 is an aggravating & exhilarating experience.

I throw stones into whirlpools.

I operate a searchlight.

The East River is turbulent.

Especially under the Hell Gate Bridge.

Police eyeball spies through my window.

I cannot write.

I must write.

I am writing.

Under constant surveillance I write in my notebook.

A novel is forthcoming.

From who?

Dunno.

Peppy Ooze?

Notebook 1 cracks me up.

I must be losing it.

Kamila.

She has incredibly long powerful

legs. She is wearing chocolate brown panties. We negotiate the room & find each other wanting. Notebook 1 is a spiral-bound notebook.

Can you see it?

Can you see the spirals?

We made choices. We made decisions. We made a movie. We made a film.

Fog. Mist. The artificial football pitch.

Somebody just baked a 500-foot-long baguette in France.

I am so hungry.

2:28 pm.

Elements of reality. Shape? Material? Plasticity? The white concrete building?

Are you losing the plot? Are you a fan of supernatural horror?

My mind frightens me.

It could turn itself off at any moment.

Then what?

Icy cold tendrils of deep outer space?

The movement of language... the film reel... the tape machine... reel-to-reel... real-to reel... reel to real... unreal to real... reel to unreal... spool & unspool... & spool again...

I am a searchlight operator.

I see everything on the Vistula!

&

The Vltava

&

The East River

I am a language man.

I am making language all the time.

Philosopher, are you reckoning?

What is your cosmic purpose?

I am a vessel for the word... I speak, I talk, I utter.

The metal stink of war.

We rummage through burned-out abandoned vehicles.

A human eyeball stares at me.

I fly no flag.
Goosebumps break out on her buttocks as she starts to come. She is lying on her belly. His hand cups her wet sex. His fingertips brush against her clitoris. His big thumb plunges in & out of her ass. "It feels so good," she murmurs. "Fuck... fuck... oh my god... FucCK FFucccghhkkkkkk!"

She gasps. Breathing hard. She

rolls onto her back. Spreads her bare legs. "Your turn," she says. Kneeling, Zig unrolls a latex over his big hard cock. He lowers himself & penetrates. Slow, smooth thrusts. She spreads a hand over his ass.

... the equilibrium between the clitoris & the cock.

A few Augenblicks later...

Thirst & hunger for loneliness?

The slowdowns & speedups during fucking.

Tight clench of ass, fingers gripping bedsheets...

We write letters.

Postcards.

Remembering & forgetting.

The video tape machine says it all... spooling & unspooling.

Be Kind Rewind.
I just live in the world. And I write about it.

So many of us lost our minds.

Erotic science fiction is all we have left.

A future metropolis.

The white concrete buildings.

Towers & fountains.

A giant telescope peeping at the Cosmos.
I wait for Ursula at the laundromat.

She is wearing a wife-beater.

Tattoos of entangled serpents on her arms.

She ignites a cigarette.

A bird's nest of dirty blond hair.

Black mascara eyes.

She laughs & pushes her panties in my face.

I throw them in the washing machine.

We start digging in our pockets for quarters.

NYC lightning.

It starts to pour.

Rain pounds the sidewalks.

Wet wet black asphalt.
Yellow cabs fly by like emergency vehicles.

Splosh & splash of deepwater puddles.

Nervous energy.

Erotic energy.

Ursula & I go back to the apartment & fuck.

She wants it doggie-style.

We do it on the fire escape.

Rain & rain & rain.

She howls.

I yelp.

Every morning I take riverwalks.

I have so much to say.

I remain silent.

I wait.
I wait for the opportunity.

The metropolis ignores me.

As it should.

I am just a creature here. A living breathing creature.

A seagull.

A pigeon.

A human being.

What makes anybody so special?

Go ahead.

Throw a rock into the East River.

Broken glass against the sea wall.

In a tidal strait, the sea ebbs & flows.

The walls of Dubrovnik.

The walls of Prague Castle.
You must ask questions if there are any?

The walker in the city.

I am tired now.

I need a drink.

A place to sit.

Possibly a tavern.

Or even just a cup of coffee.

Is it morning again?

Afternoon?

Notebook 1 is in my pocket.

A blue ink pen.

Or is it black ink?

Pilot Precise V5 or V7?

Decisions.

Decisions.
Repetitions.

The back & forth of fucking.

Fall on me... & make some noise.

Paragraphs. We need paragraphs. Where is the plot? Where is the story? Is language enough? Is language too much?

Notebook 1 is trying my patience.

Am I getting anywhere?

I feel grumpy.

It is a peculiar thing to be... a writer.

Why do you do it?!

I play das Sprachspiel.

I interrogate the 6 senses.

Perception.

Human language.

Human consciousness.

You try to grasp the plasma of spacetime.

Oozes through your fingertips.

All the teachers you ever had.

Where are they now?

Is it normal to be a person?

Are we changing?

We eclipse 4K & you expect more?

Amerika, if such a thing exists... spreads out before me... a labyrinth of cornfields... a metropolis of labyrinths.

Everything feels so ridiculous... I try to work... in a factory... it makes no sense!

The machine grinds you into sausage meat.

We throw light onto human equations.

Algorithms.

Biorhythms.

Quadratic equations.

Are you having a "private experience"?

She is fucking me in Prague and/or New York City.

She says, "How does this compare

with reality?"

What can be said?

Fog. Mist. Cloud. Rain. This is human language & human consciousness. I am ensconced in an apartment in New York City. My bones ache. My muscles are torn. I keep thinking about thinking. What am I even saying? Surveillance camera. I am either looking though it or being seen. Droplets of water on the fish-eye lens distort everything. I might be safe. Free. Unseen. A blur. The file name they have given me is Veverka, a codename. I am always at the end of the alphabet. Where I belong. On the edge of language, where meaning falls off. Is there a cliff, an abyss? I am a creature of limestone caves. The karst is in me. Dripping... drip drip drip... into stalagmites & stalactites. Mind the boatsman's hints on the underground river. Cybernetic steerer. Blip blip blip. I am a blip on somebody's computer screen. A cursor. A

profanity. My thoughts are
coming along nicely. Are you the
maker of my meaning? Are you
my keeper? The slices of apple
on a plate are a nice touch. The
iced coffee in a stainless-steel
container. I sip. I think. I sip
& think. I think I think? Am I a
thinker? Are there limits of the
language? An ex-lover pulls into
the driveway. Nervous agitation
in the bedroom. We say hi.
Everybody used to be somebody
else. What am I saying? What can
be said? I am changing. Spelling
eludes me. Grammar. The grammar
of a raw fuck in late October. It
is April, May. I am a delusion.
Sitting in front of an imaginary
computer screen. They pretend
to care: the People on the other
side. Plastic people. Elastic
people. What a flexible person I
am. I stretch & I get stretched.
Language wriggles everything
out of me. No need for an
interrogation room. I interrogate
myself. We can pretend it is
otherwise. It is fun to pretend.
We make believe & we make

believe. Repetition & difference.
I lurch & I stagger. There are
portals in the walls. Memory
holes. I can go anywhere. Prague.
New York City. Berlin. Vienna. I
prefer Astoria, Queens. There is
no here here. The Triboro Bridge
hums in 1936 & 1946 & 1956 &
1966 & 1976 & 1986 & 1996 &
2006 & 2016 & 2026 & 2036. If
this is not science-fiction, what
is? A sun throws light onto a
spinning planet. Through fog &
mist & cloud & rain. An eerie
concrete glow. Tinged with blue
& every other color that ever
was. I sip iced coffee & I think
& I think. Too much thinking gets
you where exactly? Am I ignoring
something? The flesh bucket?
The flesh machine? The forests
& marshlands of Westchester? An
osprey builds a nest. A stream
trickles over a slab of rock in
Connecticut. I make my plans
in New York City. Diagrams &
sketches. My keeper keeps an
eye on me. "Careful," she says.
"There are other people 'out
there'." Or maybe I say it. And

I persuade myself. I am a good
talker sometimes. Other times I
collapse into silence. A machine-
made silence. Noise cancellation.
We used to make noises, my ex-
lover & I. Grunts & gasps. Holy
fucks! Oh my gods! Now there is
contempt & ignorance. I serve
my sentence. I serve my time. A
second-serve, if you will. Not
"all or nothing" like going for
an ace. I make enough noise to
get by. People think I am alive.
I breathe. I snore. I hear things.
The hard slapping of ass against
thighs. Faster & faster. I wish
I could forget all the love we
made. All the pleasure of the
flesh.

I feel better & worse. Every
day is something else. The
chirp of a bird. A radio voice.
A computer voice. "Time to get
up!" somebody says. Somebody
from the Other Side. The people
of the Elsewhere. The super
elastic people. The plastic
people. I am rigid. I am hard. I
am beginning to crack. Fissures

in the eggshell of being. Fry
me up. Scramble me. Sunnyside-
up. A scream can crack an egg.
Have you ever tried? I linger
in morning. It is my wheelhouse.
My time of day. When nothing
much is happening. At least not
yet. Where everything is born.
The possibility of possibility.
Even if it is just an illusion.
Teeth get brushed. Iced coffee
gets sipped. The iris of the
surveillance camera opens. The
eyeball blinks. Augenblick. You
are beyond the edge of seeing.
A thing on the periphery. Stay
there. Try not to move. The
camera detects motion. Wait for
the eyeball to blink. It never
blinks. You must relocate. You
must recalibrate. You must change
your life! Even if you yell
at yourself. If you scream at
eternity. At the yawning abyss.
Never forget the tavern life.
There are friends there. Awaiting
your return.

I like it. Whatever is happening.
I am somebody else. My brain

has been washed. Squeaky clean.
Clouds scudding through my
consciousness. The rippled
surface of the East River.
Agitated & excited. We walk
our dogs & talk. She has an
Australian shepherd. I have a
black-mouth cur, a mongrel from
Tennessee. The dogs wrestle.
Chase each other. The girl and I,
we talk about Mattituck. She has
blue eyes & dirty blond hair. A
gray hoodie with the hoodie up.

My feet are wet from the walk.
I was wearing my leather slip-
ons. Now I am in my socks. Wet
black socks. I stare at the
computer. Getting ready to write.
The machine eyeball watches.
Looking over my left shoulder.
Is the information useful? What
facts have you gathered? What
evidence? What meaning are you
making?

This might be a stand-alone
piece.

This might go into Notebook 1.

I was thinking & talking about Route 25A in the summer with that girl. I was saying how crowded it gets nowadays. Like just as bad as the Hamptons. Though not really.

The North Fork is the North Fork.

Like when Einstein sent a letter from Cutchogue to FDR about the atomic bomb.

Is a story emerging from Notebook 1? I have no idea. I am just a recorder. I operate with signs. I am an operator of signs. A sign operator.

I hope not.

I hope we go beyond story.

Into the margins of the margins of yr mind.

I stare at walls

&

walls stare back.

System creep... oozing into your livingroom through the telescreen.

Not sure why I live here... or why I live anywhere.

Circumstance.

Happenstance.

A mere fortuity.
The browngray sky & a storm lurks...

Neon green trees...

The atomic attack came out of nowhere. As we always knew it would. There was no time to "duck & cover". Even less time to think. People ran in circles. Raided supermarkets. Asked the bartender for another round. Even the sports teams on the TV kept playing. One last bucket. One last goal. I tried to make a telephone call on a payphone.

Until I remembered no one does that anymore. Besides, the line was dead.

I wake up in a lunatic asylum. Why not. Feels right. The nurse asks me to take my pill. I want to play basketball in the courtyard. I want to go fishing on the high seas. Everything happens so fast.

Life is fast.

I take out the garbage & recycling.

Night gets scarier & scarier.

You ask big questions.

It is not something you can squeeze into a camera.

Notebook 1 needs to get bigger. This is ridiculous. You and your microscripts. Grow a pair. Write something.

I was surrounded by migrants in the parking lot of a Home Depot.

They wanted to steal my chairs.

Or they wanted to help me put my chairs into the car.

For money.

I was confused.

I was scared.

This summer is turning out to be quite an adventure.
Here it comes.

The summer.

I hope I get laid.

Notebook 1 just goes on & on and no one gives a fuck.

Are you still here?

Why?

Go watch Netflix or something.

I am supposed to play in a football game tonight. Will

Spiros pass the ball? Will Rachel be there?

Our goalkeeper Ian is out. Family emergency in Massachusetts.

Am I a memoirist?

Am I a novelist?

This is my brain on a wire.

I am taking a readout.
I apologize.

You are here for the ride.

After a football match, I am crystal clear.

I see through myself.

I see the cosmos.

Nothing is happening. I must make it happen. I am making it happen right now.

Experiments.

Mind games.

A novel.

A reality text.

You there... are you participating? Are you a thread in the fabric?

Are you satisfied with your situation?

Your role?

Notebook 1 is a period in the mind.

Today, for example, is the 21st of May.

In other words, Tuesday.

The year is whatever year it is.

The refrigerator is making noise.

Ice in the diffuser.

The styrofoam & plastic box

between the freezer & the refrigerator.

My problems are your problems.

The noise stopped.

Did you fix it?

With your mind?!

I appreciate it.

I need to shave.

I need a woman to yank off my knickers.

Am I making enough noise?

The tip of her tongue electrified my cock.

I lay there.

My jeans unbuttoned.

Her ass was slick with sweat. She wanted to fuck me & I let her. She bounced that ass. Nipples erect. Cone-shaped breasts. Not sure what she told her American boyfriend. I was just a phase. I did not exist. I was a phantom ghost.

What is happening with you on the 27th of May? The fog. The mist. Splashing through pooling agua on the Grand Central Parkway.

You motor vehicle is a Toyota. Yes? What is wrong with the battery? The starter?

Is seltzer keeping you going?

How long?

I rode the Q69 bus today. What a ride. I might ride a bicycle with the old car battery in a basket. To get a new car battery. I feel like Thoreau or something.

Is the car battery dead? Is it really dead?

What if it is the starter?

I am angry at the Universe.

Entropy.

What did I expect?

Negentropy?

My thoughts are jotted down for your perusal. Are they similar to your thoughts? Totally different? Are they echoes? Are you familiar with a secret agent named Igor?

I am keeping an eyeball on Igor.

Making notes & whatnot.

Igor is a rogue operator.

The worst kind.

The easiest & hardest to track.

So obviously there & not.

A phantom.

A glimpse.

Augenblick.

I was at the Costco warehouse today. What a disaster. They did not have the right car battery. I almost got stranded in the parking lot. Crank crank crank. False start. No start. Finally, enough of a spark for a mini-explosion of gasoline in a gasoline engine.
I puttered away. Thanking the Jesus.

Janet & I crucified each other. Upside down. She had my cock in her mouth, and I had her cunt in my mouth. We gave each other everything there was to give.

This happened in the dormitories of Saint Rose.

I am made of wild thoughts in the wilderness.

The city streets tried to civilize me.

Failure.

If anything, the metropolis made we wilder.

Radical.

A rogue operator.

Not unlike Igor, who I keep in the crosshairs of my machine eyeball.
Beware, Igor.

Beware!

This notebook is getting out of hand.

The machine is taking over.

Artificial consciousness.

Is anything possible anymore?

Are we just knee-jerk reactions?

I need to make music. The silence is killing me. Literature is for the lunatics. Literature is for the People of the Bughouse.

Notebook 1 is a book of Nothingness.

I empty words of meaning.

The next day is the day after yesterday.

I was surrounded by Somalis in a parking lot. They wanted to help me.

I bought chairs.

Clear plastic bags.

Everybody is wandering the planet. Looking for something.

Amerika is a sprawling facility.

ameri(K)a
... a sort of pseudo-reality

Apartment no. 18

We make love in the semi-darkness. Five children are born. A sixth after I return from prison. There is BEFORE & there is AFTER. Before the after is the PRESENT TENSE. The hardest space to occupy. To live. Everything happens so fast... too fast... & not fast enough. All the information is here. I record the data in a notebook. Read it if you must.

Install this anti-novel... this anti-reality... make it burn eyeballs & default settings & brainwashed minds!

Defect.

Or stay behind.

Totalitarianism is a memoir I have yet to write.

American eel in the East River.

The carnies in a carnival are installing the joy machines in a parking lot across the street.

I am going to lose my mind.

Is it possible to live like a human being?

Mr. Zbran wants to talk to you.

Shall I say you are available?

Are your thoughts imported from elsewhere?

I write a novel under constant surveillance.

She cannot get my pants off fast enough. She wants my flesh inside her. Carnal knowledge.

She asks me questions. Interrogates.

I am in trouble this month.

I have no income.

I await the trickle of the future.

Is she coming?

Am I coming?

What do you tolerate in silence?

Havel says the regime "pretends to pretend nothing."

Report to the Sub-Ulterior Minister at the Ministry of the Ulterior.

We must investigate the stellar perturbations & tidal effects of the Oort Cloud.

Say yes.

Say yes to life.

Celebrate.

Is there enough rain left in the atmosphere?

Are you cooling off?

Chilling out?

The pocket machine is an anxiety device.

Shut it down.

Throw it into the fishpond.

Am I happening?

Are we happening?

I write sentences.

Separated by whitespace.

That is, it.

Nothing else.

Your journal entry intrigues me.

Adjunct lecturer.

Are you listening?

Everybody loves a story.

Everybody loves a performance.

I walked the dog this morning. I overheard a woman say it was an election year. She was going to go to Wisconsin & Chicago. She also said not much campaigning was happening. Trump was in court for a month. She asked me how old my dog was. I said nine months.

I thought I might like to fuck this woman. Really fuck her. Make her come on the tip & base of my cock. Doggie-style.

I write this under police surveillance.

Trefry says: Write like no one is watching.

We need to make some rules.

Are you familiar with the Soviet bloc countries?

We emerge from a concrete hi-rise apartment block.

Is there at least a small

balcony?

Are you aware of the political reality?

What are your political impulses?

I want to live like a human being.

Are you of an "undesirable political background"?

Are you in the Index of Undesirable Persons under the codename FUNKY GOULET?

I fixed the bathroom sink today. There was a long gelatinous schlong in the pipe clogging things up.

What tram have you taken to "the end of the line"?

Is there a roundabout?

Or do the tracks just disappear into infinity?

A vanishing point.

Beware of the Soviet black Volga.

We were slowly gliding lovers... laying & getting laid...

Are you listening to Bee Gees?

Are you familiar with Soviet leader Leonid Brezhnev?

To write is to dissent... enough is enough... I want more!

ZIG: Check!
KAMILA: Checkmate!

We are fucking.

She has that delicious blond ass.

Are you satisfied with your "lived experience"?

Are you craving?

Oranges?

Lemons?

Bananas?

Are we Writing People?

The secret police searched
the apartment again. I was in
my underwear. I really really
wanted to sleep. They found
no illegal manuscripts. I have
writer's block, I said. It happens
to all of us.

Are we Dog People?

Are we People of the Dog?

We walk our dogs in the park.
Surveillance vans parked near
the bodega. Agents eating bacon,
egg, & cheese on a roll, SPK.

Salt.
Pepper.
Ketchup.

Rachel asks for doggie-style.

I oblige.

The news today is oblivion.

Radio & TV.

TV apocalypse.

Blonde with a tattoo. Totally my cup of čaj.

I need more information.

mem(o)ry h(o)le
...a n(o)vel

The sun pulses a distorted blood-orange h(o)le in the sky. It is an uncertain thing. A throbbing ball of fiery plasma. And yet we take it for granted. Assume it will do what it always did. I am a little more skeptical than most. And sometimes I wonder.

I record things. I have no other purpose. Reactions. Thoughts. I have the basic language. Emotions. Desires. I ride the surface of the planet like everybody else. Spinning & orbiting & corkscrewing through the galaxy.

There are spaces between the spaces. You cannot see it. They are invisible. Abstract. A numerical equation. An algorithm. We no longer think fast enough. Leave the thinking to the machines.

I pretend to be a human being. It suits my purposes.

Purposeless purpose.

Beware of purple prose!

The machine investigates the anomalies. Are you an anomaly? Or are you like everybody else? Think twice before you answer.

My job is to make things happen. I open the memory holes. They are portals. They are vacuums. They will suck the air out of you. The breath. Keep breathing while you can.

Prison is a funny place. Time

stands still in a cell. Are you a potential candidate?

Are you a writer?

We despise writers. They take themselves so seriously.

Laugh a little.

Fuck a woman. Fuck a man.

Get out of your room!

Cigarettes & beer. Your belly on the small of the back of a woman you used to love.

Howl.

Speak.

We lurch towards Gomorrah. We lurch towards Sodom.

Amerika is on fire!

Europe is on fire!

I can't be left to my own devices.

Otherwise.

Nothing gets done.

Yes... yes... open another mem(o)ry h(o)le. See what happens.

We might end up elsewhere.

Or nowhere.

Spacetime lingers in the echo chamber.

The machines are talking & I can't quite follow.

Yeah... I'm feelin' feelin' feelin'... kind of hollow.

Zig & Kamila
...another friggin novel by r.g. vasicek

Asymmetrical blond bangs & cult-like green eyes. She likes the thickness of my dick. Fills her up, so to speak, she tells her girlpals. Almost like a gasoline filling station. Yes, Amerika is like that. We are all dissidents. Because dissent is the American way. Ask George Washington. Ask Ben Franklin. Ask Henry David Thoreau.

The metropolis lures us in like a honeytrap. The tall buildings. The alleyways. The century-old pubs & taverns. The People of the Suburbs are suckers for such & sundry. At least I learn to do my laundry in a laundromat.

Kamila has the best ass in Texas. She brings it up to New York in a VW Beetle. Parks it on Park Avenue before she finds a place in the East Village. She meets Zig in a laundromat. He begs her for quarters & laundry detergent. She is a woman's woman, for sure. All tits & ass.

I am a little dumb, for a boy. I pretend I am smarter. I figure out that if you stare into space long enough, people figure you for a prophet. I use every weapon I can get. I want to be a writer. A novelist.

I keep switching between third-person & first-person. I am very confused.

Amerika has its grip on me. I ain't going anywhere.

Kamila & Zig keep each other occupied in the metropolis. They get jobs as ushers at a theater. People really do not need help finding their seats. Sometimes they tip. Sometimes not. Zig & Kamila see some of the best actors & actresses in Amerika go through that theater.

Zig wants to write a play. Kamila wants to be a star.

How did I get into this mess? This mess of being a writer. It really is chaos in here, here being in the space of my mind. Not enough elbow room, is there?

We do our thing. We do our time. The metropolis swirls & swirls &

swirls.

Kamila & Zig know a couple named Fritz & Marnie. They do everything together. Party together. Sometimes even sleep together. One never really knows whose dick is in who. The kayak trip on the Mississippi is the best. They figure they should swap partners for a while.

Alas! Life is not forever.

Amerika... of all places... of course... of course...

The self-forgetting necessary for a successful fuck.

Underground seminar.

Are you ready? Are we ever?

I leave Kamila & Zig behind. Let them fornicate.

Welcome to the space of becoming.

A risky path awaits you, writer...

Uncertainty.

Ambiguity.

Mystery.

The unknowable thing-in-itself.

Are you a speaker of Attic Greek in the metropolis of Athens?

We drink radioactive water.

We work in the uranium mines at Camp Nikolai.

The landscape is in ruins.

Wasteland.

Upsurge.

We are thinkers at the bottom.

Diagnosis 307.

Kurvafix!

Yamaha RZ-350... žlutý like a yellow-jacket.

Klinovsky!

Tarkovsky!

We reemerge from the Zone.

The machine parts in our wheelbarrows are beyond compare.

A German shepherd lies next to me in a puddle.

Amerika intoxicates.

The 7-Eleven in Ronkonkoma is where we get our coffee.

I can smell the L.I.E.

I can hear it.

Mojmír is a good name for an anti-hero.

Are you listening?

Are you fearless?

I wander the streets of New York City. Where is the tram to

Holešovice? No name is good enough for me. I am Zig. I zig & zag. The N train & its funky route.

The State does not require all of you.

Only a part of you.

Enough to show your acquiescence.

The hand-crank pencil sharpener screwed into a plank of wood. The recessed LED ceiling lights in the kitchen. The mason jar of quarters & nickels & pennies. The Japanese acoustic guitar leaning against a wall of red brick & glass cubes. Morning light from the nearest star oozes into the apartment.

On weekends you wander the gravel trail around Lake Minnewaska in the Shawnagunks.

Are your thoughts intact?

Aired out by mountain breeze?

You pilot the Toyota across the George Washington Bridge onto Harlem River Drive.

The Triboro Bridge.

Astoria Boulevard.

Wherever you go, be there thoroughly.

A laptop pops open on your lap. A machine is made.

Petite machines for the immigrant proletariat.

And the petit bourgeois.

Are you a French speaker? Are you a Czech speaker? Are you an American speaker?

Is language your language?

Are you Writing People?

Are we industrializing the

language?

Diagnosis 307.

Are we underground? I think so.
I hope so. If they find us, they
crush us. We are just people.
Trying to be people. I like
what I am saying so far. Feels
right. Feels true. Language is a
crapshoot. We take our chances.
See what happens.

The metropolis is exhilarating.
So many places to hide. I was
in a movie theater last night. I
could've been anybody. A random
person. Kamila was there, too.
She pretended not to know me.
I pretended not to know her.
Strangers.

Nobody cares about paragraphs
anymore. I still find them useful.
If only to break things up.
Simplify. Things are already so
complicated. Feelings. Emotions.
Logic. It is all a super freaky
fandango if you ask me.

I wake up in cold sweats. A
hard-on like the Statue of
Liberty. The Empire State
Building. No woman in my bed.
Kamila is sleeping with somebody
else. I don't mind. It was time,
I guess. Everybody wants an
adventure.

I think my best thoughts alone.
No one else to think them for
me. I read books. I watch movies.
That's about it. Sometimes I
listen to music.

Washing dishes is peaceful. A
sense of accomplishment. I can
control the world from a kitchen
sink. I can shape reality. I rinse
the forks & the spoons & the
knives.

What is on TV? Nothing much.
Just the propaganda. The screen
tries to suck your face in. Best
to turn it off. I would get rid of
it. If it was not a requirement.

I live in a building. A five-
story building. There are ten

apartments. I live on the top floor. Apartment # 9.

There is no elevator. I climb the stairs. Keeps my ass in shape. I might need it, if I ever meet another woman. Kamila said I had a delicious ass. Best to forget those days. Best to forget those nights. It is me against the metropolis. The metropolis is my friend.

I am not a writer. I am a thinker. Is there a difference? I think my thoughts. I write them down.

There are walls of notebooks in my apartment. Every now & again, I take one down. Notebooks # 1. Notebook # 68. Notebook number # 137. It will end when it ends.

The tram is not far from here. How could it be otherwise? I cross the tram tracks. I wait in a kiosk. The # 22 takes me almost everywhere I need to go. There are probably places I need to go that I do not know. Everything in due course. Or, better yet, surprise me.

Life is atomic. I feel the orbit inside me. Outside me. Gravity waves play their games. Make their music. I am a vessel floating in the aether. I am eager for the ride. The cataracts & the waterfalls. The whirlpools.

There is a little truth in everything you say. So, if you speak, you get to know yourself. Otherwise? Oblivion. Silence hurts like a motherfucker in the industrial precincts of Brno.

I once wore a Nike T-shirt on a street next to a factory. A teenage hooligan on the other side of the street yelled: "Nike! Now that is a shirt!"

I felt like an imbecile.

Never again!

I had to become less & less. So I could become more & more.

More emptiness, please.

More nothingness.

I kiss the abyss.

I spent time with the machine poets of Ronkonkoma. They made improbable industrial music. They smashed sledgehammers & giant adjustable wrenches against cold steel. They hid their human faces behind medieval welding masks. They built contraptions that would one day conquer the world.

Here we are again. Getting ready for a football match. I have no desire to play. And yet I play. Just to see what happens.

2-2 is the final score.

The artificial green turf. The floodlights. The breeze from the East River.

I can relax. For whatever reason, they removed the police

surveillance eyeball.

I grew up in a machine shop. The machine shop grew up in me. We raised each other. Wild metal & flesh.

My hands smell like kitchen sponge. I am thinking about the cosmos. How big is it? Bigger than big? Every day is a kaleidoscope. The time is 9:35 AM. Whatever that means. 9:36 because I type so slow. I am typing. Typing is thinking.

Let the naysayers say nay all they want.

I say yes.

Say yes to the sparrow.

Are you banging away on a 1905 Perkeo writing machine?

Made in Dresden.

Schreibmaschine.

Maschinenfabrik.

Ja ja ja.

I write because I write.

Is Prague a maze or a labyrinth?

Is NYC a Chinese fingertrap?

Am I trapped in the trap of the trap?

It was a Moravian summer. We had our pants off all summer. I gave her cunnilingus & she reciprocated. She had a good head on her shoulders. I really loved her ass.

Now.

I am bored.

She is twenty-two. Or twenty. A lifeguard at the swimming pool. "Are you okay, Sir?" she asks, after I emerge. I had finished my twelve laps with a kickboard. Perhaps I struggled? Do I appear winded? "Worried?" I smile, "I am okay. First time swimming in six months." (More probably, almost a year). She has nice hair. Nice legs. Perhaps she is just trying to engage me in conversation. I feel thankful. Energized.

I will think about the lifeguard for a long time, I think.

What next, Sir?

Are you a graybeard?

Not yet.

A writer lurks at the perimeter of reality.

The ferry ride on the East River calms my nervous system.

Quick! A glass of iced coffee.

Back inside the apartment: the indoor thermometer reads 89 degrees Fahrenheit.

I sip!

I make faces at the Universe.

I make my way into the aether.

Thicker & deeper than ever before.

My thoughts are humid.

A plasma.

Oozing into thoughts of other thoughts.

Easy on the hajzlpapir.

So much to ponder.

Experience, thoughts, & feelings... the psychological richness... the narrative drama of the infidel... the affair... sex is a happening... a phenomenon... phenomena... a ritual... experiment & deviation... repetition & difference...

The Czechoslovakian State Security Police searches your apartment. Are you satisfied? Did you find what you are looking for?

Zig's interrogation file contains...

The writer knows no shame.

Not true. Not true. The writer knows shame. The writer is shame.

Prague & Brno is a network of acquaintances.

People who... know... each other.

Name recognition.

Familiarity.

Reputation.

The Writing People are a peculiar people.

Are you going to sign it?

Sign what?

You know.

The thing.

It's a mess, really. This existence.

We must do something.

Change.

Language, yes, what about it? I am trying to speak.

The Trabant farts its way into the labyrinth of Brno... a surveillance squadron in a slow agonizing pursuit...

Are you an American?

Heat wave in the Bronx.

Kids making fun of my job as an adjunct lecturer.

The writer knows shame.

My wife wants me to search the utility closet for swiffers.

And God says to Adam, "For dust

you are, and to dust you shall return."

I am a footballer.

A center back.

A sweeper.

Here comes some storm & you are unprepared.

Summer rain. I'm not afraid.

The crime of the subversion of the republic...

Thoughts & behavior...

Yes yes... there you go... at the speed of sound... & you want to go faster... faster & faster... the speed of light... faster!

The Trees?!

The trees in the city park are listening devices. I expect a few micr(o)eyeballs screwed into the bark. So I walk & think

my thoughts under constant
surveillance. Are the birds fake?
Petite automatons? Are you real,
dear reader, somewhere in the
dark of your apartment? Are you
an apartment dweller? Are we not
all denizens of a metropolis?
I suspect my metropolis is
bigger than your metropolis.
Among other things. We speak &
talk into machines. We lose our
minds. Everywhere the nowhere.
Are you satisfied with your
existence? Is it thrilling? The
swerve of life. One never really
knows what to expect. Despite
our blueprints, our plans. I
studied law. Now look at me.
What am I? I have no idea. I
might say samizdat writer. Even
that is up for grabs. I have yet
to publish my thoughts. They
linger in notebooks & closets
& drawers. Haunting thoughts,
really. I am terrified of
myself. The monster inside. I am
rightfully under surveillance.
The creature such that I am.
Wanting. Lusting. Desiring.
Throw me a few bread rolls.

Perhaps an aluminum-wrapped triangle of cheese. I might smoke a cigarette. I might sip a beer. All these possibilities are in me. And more. I type it all up on a typewriter. And the pages get hidden away. Which begs the question. How did you get a copy of this? Are you secret police? Are you an ex-lover? Are you a potential employer? If the latter, I must warn you: I am unemployable. If you are an ex-lover, I suspect we have both moved on. Finding ourselves beneath others, crying out into the Cosmos. The pages pile up. The trees listen for a century or more. There are trees that are a thousand years old. Every book is an ancient tree. Are you a keeper of books? Is there a petrified forest in your apartment? What brings it to life? You? Speak! Talk! Your mind is an amphitheater. An echo chamber. A bughouse.

I pause because I too am ancient. I need rest. I need calm. I am restless & anxious & nervous. So much life courses through me... a river of whirlpools & cataracts. There are people out there trying to digitize me. Are they insane? I am made of ink & paper. I am made of human soul. I want. And I need. The thought of a woman's naked ass against my belly. If only to sleep at night.

The flesh. The spirit. I am made of madness. I am making things up as I go along. Every writer takes a breath. Inhale. Exhale. Spit it out if you can.

Not everybody's shit smells like cinnamon, I'll say that... & rolls & rolls of toilet paper are made from ancient trees... & we unscroll our thoughts... spool & unspool... & the outhouses cannot take it anymore... & the raccoons attack from the ancient forest... armed with bows & arrows & crossbows & mace...

I jumped into a three-wheeled motorcar to make my escape... a two-stroke microcar... & I did wheelies in the metropolis... if only to catch the attention of the secret police... & I led them deeper & deeper into the labyrinth...

Police helicopter circles my apartment building... I deserve it... the machine noise... the whirlybird... I might play football tomorrow night... let the coppers stand on the edge of the artificial turf pitch... agog

I am a mango for life... there is no retiring... the Iron Curtain!

So much noise in the metropolis. So much circumstance. Here comes the helicopter again. Is the pilot not satisfied?

Yes. I exist. I am here.

The dog people on the hill mull about & talk. Klamm is begging for treats.

I keep a toe on the perimeter.

A breeze snarls through the trees.

Ameri(K)a is getting bigger & bigger.

Back at the apartment, our fucking became more diverse in style & tone. Kamila wanted to come. And come she did. Even if it meant inviting neighbors to participate.

The written traces of a lover...

So nervous about football tonight... why?

Can't find my cleats.

Fuck it.

I am teaching a summer class this summer. Composition. Are you a composer?

What is writing?

Why do I write?

Last night I dreamed that I was fucking my wife doggie-style... about time, I thought... the dream was interrupted... I awoke disappointed.

For some reason I am thinking about Eva.

The missed opportunity at the Paper Hotel.

We both lament, perhaps?

Julian was released from prison yesterday.

I don't even know what meaning means anymore.

We are up against everything.

Man v. Everything.

The heat wave is over, I think.

At least for now.

A strange breeze blew in from the west.

Might go shopping at Lidl.
Watermelons are in season.

What now... if.

I get it.

A lot is at stake.

Danielle & I are fucking in the office one day. She is a writer, too. So I am fair game. She knows what she wants. Knows how to get it. My skull in the vice-grip of her thighs. She wiggles a finger into me.

I must have squirted a bucket of semen into her & still she did not get pregnant.

July is on the horizon.

I am terrified.

We roll into the beer hall like bowling balls, knocking everybody over. "Get me a beer! Get me a beer!" Danielle jumps on the bar & performs a Scottish jig.

Def Leppard roaring on the jukebox. Pyromania!

Friday. Saturday. Sunday. The weekends are endless. I stare at rocks on the beach.

The sea smirks.

The surveillance van in the parking lot pulls out & speeds away.

I see you!

I shake my fist.

I am a writer, dammit.

Let me write.

Maybe I am something else.

What else is there?

My fucking mind... is all over the place... a swamp thing... a creature from the pine barrens... the Neanderthal caves of Moravia

Marriage is a bordello...

The silver Tatra 87 is parked in front of the Czechoslovak embassy in Melbourne.

Australia is a bewilderment.

Kafka is in the Outback.

A desert of the real.

1st of July.

Too fucking tired.

Foucault can go fuck himself.

Baudrillard.

Husserl.

Patočka.

I want something else.

Engineers of the human soul.

Did you lock the door. Did you lock your mind?

All the ass cracks we licked in the metropolis.

Danielle elongates her tongue.

I am a retired footballer.

No more football!

I plan to run for President.

Or the Prime Minister.

Or whatever the fuck it is.

Me & Sailor & Lulu.

Danielle will be my Minister of Interior.

Zappa for Minister of Culture.

Say no to Ed Sheeran!

Yes to Billie Eilish.

The Fourth Wall got kicked in on Game of Thrones.

We are the Fourth Estate.

Rogue operators.

Rogue warriors.

Artists & machine poets.

We are Dr. Who.

The 241st episode "Heaven Sent" starring Peter Capaldi imprisoned in a waterlocked castle is particularly compelling.

I am bored by everything else.

Except for maybe the comic Swamp Thing by Alan Moore.

Issue # 34!

Are we capable of more?!

I am almost impossible.

The odds are against it.

Yet here I am.

The talking prison.

Talk talk talk.

What if I can't talk?

What if we cannot talk?

"Woman... your panties... may I remove them?"

"Yes... you may."

I remember her pussy in my face & my cock in her mouth... & we forgot about supercapitalism for a brief while... & the enormity of the metropolis... Prague & Berlin & NYC & everywhere else

We came in each other's faces.

Did you get nominated for a Pushcart Prize?

Easy on the sushi.

Wasabi is green-painted horseradish.

Am I a person?

I forget.

Are you in Dubrovnik again?

Are the walls high enough to protect you?

The language strings itself into string theory.

We walk the tightrope.

The spider web.

Taut.

Reverberations.

A tingling of the spine.

Enjoy your corpus callosum. It is a shaft of nerves in your brain.

Are you a lefty or a righty?

What are you doing at a gasoline station in Obetz, Ohio?

Pumping gas, I guess.

West 78 to Evansville, Indiana.

She told me a story & I almost fainted from laughter.

A snake at my left ankle.

Yes, yes. Amerika. Look at it.

Writer, write.

There is no other task at hand. You must bang out the language. Thumb through it. Remember everything.

I make no sense unless I am writing.

I am plugged into a writing machine.

I used to think I was possible. And then I realized I was impossible.

A vortex of emotions & electrical energy.

A vector of being.

The micr(o)phone in your pocket
is recording your existence.

The pilsner swirls in your belly
& you see a bigger cosmos.

I have nothing to say other than
my text.

So read it & scream.

Writing gets me into trouble.

I have no other plan.

"Thoughts" on a page.

I say... woman!... get those
panties off... we need to make
some moonshine!

& we forget about
supercapitalism for a while...

Asscracks in industrial cities.

The supergravity of the
metropolis luring me back in.

Lamplighter fish in an aquarium.

I am wary.

I-69 South towards the Ohio River.

What am I doing here?

Anywhere.

Write at your most vulnerable.

When everything is collapsing.

You no longer exist.

There is just... everything else.

Might go to Jiffy Lube.

The Toyota needs it.

I need it.

.8 miles to N Green River Rd, motherfucker!

I am in the cleavage of Indiana.

Writers, write. Are you a writer? Are you Writing People?

A text-based human experience.

You, Tobias. Up there in yr Parisian garret!

You, Armand. Up there in the Castle of Golemgrad. Or in the subterranean dungeons.

Are you experiencing political entropy?

Are you experiencing the everyday wanderings of a human mind?

What thoughts are thinkable?

What thoughts are left unsaid?

We approach 5K as if it matters.

We can go on forever.

The liquid self... the memory fragments... the magic juice... keeps us together

Who is this for?

Who is the audience?

I keep rewriting myself.

Erasing.

I like your nowhereness.

The cleavage of yr buttocks.

Erect cocks & swollen cunts.

A pinch of salt.

The cornfields of Indiana & Kentucky & Ohio & West Virginia.

Tornado warnings.

Shelter in basement.

Shelter in a metropolis.

Shelter in NYC.

Shelter in Prague.

103 degrees Fahrenheit.

Are you satisfied?

The brutal architecture of the future.

The mind wanderers are telepathic.

Long-distance interrogations.

Are you alert?

Emergency people.

You realize that Pepsi-Cola is iced coffee.

Did you make a pitstop in Pittsburgh?

I miss that blond-ass woman from Monroeville.

She treated me just right.

Who is afraid of Kathy Acker in Amerika?

The hamburger joints of Amerika...

She has incandescent conical tits. An ass like Cleopatra.

Her ass in Zig's hands; her cunt on his cock. She & Zig grunt in raw pleasure.

Sex is anxiety.

Anxiety is sex.

Anxious to copulate.

Eager.

The Dr. promises Tadalafil will provide firmer erections & a "wet ejaculation" as opposed to the dry cum of Tamsulosin.

My prostate is the size of a grapefruit.

Do I exaggerate?

Do I ejaculate?

Are we "under surveillance" among friends?

Did you really watch the 1973 flick The Day of the Jackal?

Are you a radio journalist?

Are you listening?

I don't feel very good Amerika is too big & I eat Tums to keep the acid out of my mouth

I lay under a blond-ass Pittsburgh biker chick with tattoos & watch her shimmy up & down my wet fat cock... I flip her over for the grunting... she says she wants to eat a subway sandwich later... with horseradish I say

I am not going anywhere I tell myself & it feels good to say the truth & not eat up all the TV lies about getting better & better

I like the nobodiness of it all...

I always wonder what people are thinking about me & they are not thinking anything at all

She eats that sandwich like she

is really hungry & I think she is

I can see the blond cunt hairs
poking out of the crotch of her
panties

We both spread our legs & wonder
who is going to fuck who

The past never really gets
resolved and just keeps on going
& going

It is 2:54am I am probably
writing on a typewriter

I walk the dog to take a piss
& nobody murders me I think
because people love dogs

The novel is never really ready
is it

Printed in Great Britain
by Amazon